COYOTE
SINGS TO THE MOON

COYOTE
SINGS TO
THE MOON

Thomas King
ILLUSTRATED BY Johnny Wales

Key Porter Kids

Library and Archives Canada Cataloguing in Publication

King, Thomas, 1943-
  Coyote sings to the moon / Thomas King ; illustrated by Johnny Wales.

ISBN 1-55013-946-0 (bound).--ISBN 978-1-55263-868-2 (pbk.)

  I. Wales, Johnny II. Title.

PS8571.I5298C69 1998   jC813'.54   C97-932058-5

The publisher gratefully acknowledges the support of the Canada Council for the Arts and the Ontario Arts Council for its publishing program. We acknowledge the support of the Government of Ontario through the Ontario Media Development Corporation's Ontario Book Initiative.

We acknowledge the financial support of the Government of Canada through the Book Publishing Industry Development Program (BPIDP) for our publishing activities.

KPk is an imprint of
Key Porter Books Limited
Six Adelaide Street East, Tenth Floor
Toronto, Ontario
Canada M5C 1H6

www.keyporter.com

Design: Jean Lightfoot Peters

Printed and bound in Canada

08 09 10 11 12 5 4

For Elizabeth and Benjamin, who think Coyote's singing got a bum rap
T. K.

To my sisters and brother, Morna, Sally, and David,
I affectionately dedicate this book
J. W.

long time ago, before animals stopped talking to human beings, Old Woman lived in a woods by a pond. And every evening, she walked down to the pond and waited for the moon to come up.

In those days, the moon was much closer to the earth and the light from the moon was much brighter. And when the full moon rose above the trees, Old Woman sang out in a strong voice, "Moon, Moon, full Moon."

And when the moon was a half moon, she sang, "Moon, Moon, half Moon."

And when it was a crescent, she sang, "Moon, Moon, crescent Moon."

One evening, all the animals in the woods came down to the pond just to hear Old Woman sing to the moon.

"What a beautiful voice," say the moose.

"Yes," say the ducks, "but we need a livelier beat."

"And a little cool percussion," say the beavers, ba-dopity-bop-bopping their tails on the water.

"Doo-wop, doo-wop," say the turtles and the frogs.
"Don't forget the harmony."
So, one by one, all the animals join in with Old Woman and sing to the moon.
"Moon, Moon, full Moon."

One evening, Coyote hears Old Woman and the animals singing to the moon.

"Pardon me," says Coyote, smiling his Coyote smile. "Exactly what are you doing?"

"We're singing to Moon," says Old Woman.

"Well," says Coyote, taking out his comb and brushing his coat, checking his teeth with his tongue, and wiping his nose on his arm. "What you need is a good tenor."

"No! No!" shout all the animals. "You have a terrible singing voice!"

"Yes," says Old Woman. "Your voice could scare Moon away."

"Hummph," says Coyote, whose feelings are hurt. "Why would anyone want to sing to Moon, anyway?"

"Moon is our friend," says Old Woman. "She travels all over the world just so we can have light at night."

"Who wants light at night?" says Coyote. "That silly Moon is so bright, I can hardly sleep. Why, I wouldn't sing with you if you begged me."

Now, Moon hears Coyote, and, the more she listens, the angrier she gets.

"Okay," she says to herself, "let's see how Coyote likes it dark."

And she packs her bags, slides out of the sky, and dives down into the pond.

When Moon dives into the pond, the whole world gets really bright.

"Hey!" says Coyote. "How come it's so bright?"

And then it gets really dark.

"Hey!" says Coyote. "How come it's so dark?"

And when Old Woman and Coyote stop arguing to catch their breath and they look up in the sky, they see that Moon is gone.

"This is your fault," says Old Woman. "Moon must have heard your bad thoughts."

"Well," says Coyote. "at least now I can get some sleep."

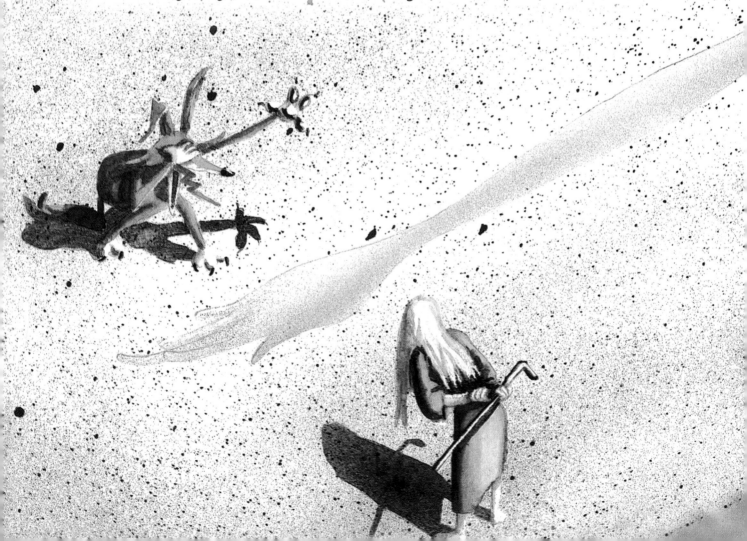

As soon as Coyote leaves, Old Woman calls the animals together.

"We have to find Moon and get her to go back into the sky," says Old Woman, "or this world is going to be messed up."

"But where would Moon go?" says Moose.

"I don't know," says Old Woman. "But we better start looking."

So all the animals and Old Woman begin searching through the dark for Moon.

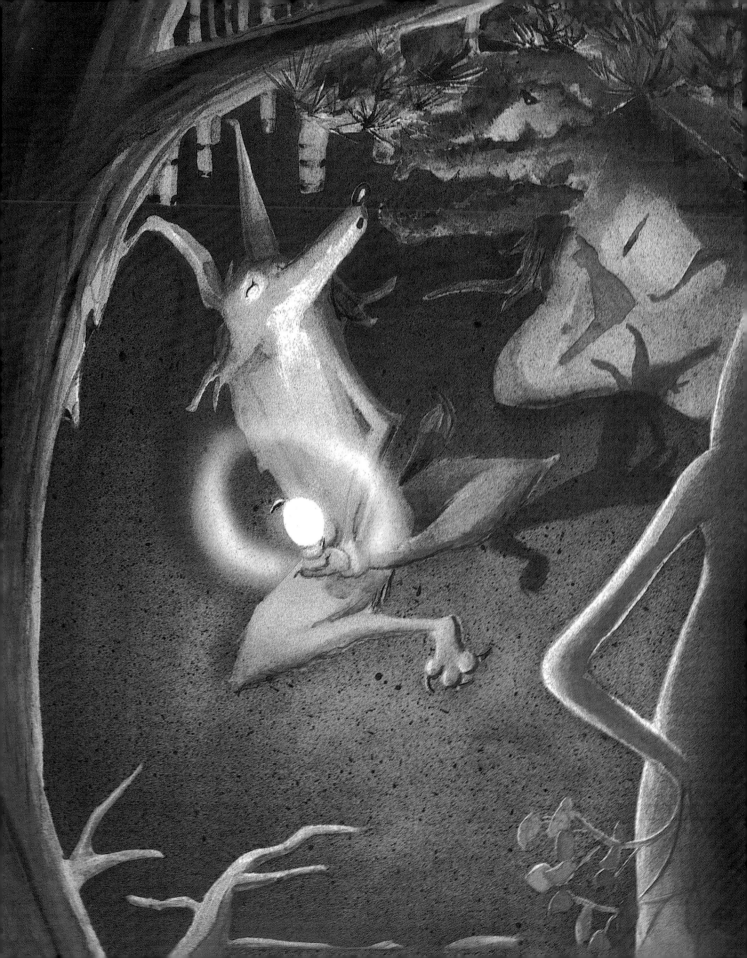

While the animals and Old Woman are searching, Coyote is trying to find his way home.

"I think it's in this direction," says Coyote, and he walks into a tree.

"Hey!" says Tree. "Watch where you're going."

"Sorry," says Coyote, "but it's dark."

"That's because some fur-brain insulted Moon," says Tree, "and she has gone away."

"I can see just fine," says Coyote, and he walks into a large boulder.

"I'll bet that hurt," says Boulder.

"Ouch," says Coyote. "I'm trying to find my way home."

"Sure could use a little Moonlight," says Boulder.

"Never mind," says Coyote.

Coyote tries to feel his way in the dark, but he keeps bumping into trees and rocks and keeps slipping on wet moss and tripping over sneaky roots.

"Maybe I should just sleep here tonight," says Coyote, "and go home in the morning."

Coyote feels around and finds a nice flat spot, and he feels around some more and finds something soft and warm.

"This will make a cozy pillow," says Coyote, as he fluffs up the soft and warm thing and puts it under his head.

Just as Coyote is falling asleep, the pillow begins to move.

"Stop that," says Coyote. "I'm trying to sleep."

"So am I," says the pillow.

Coyote can't see a thing, but his nose tells him that he may have made a big mistake. Coyote sniffs a little here and he sniffs a little there.

"I hope you're a cuddly sack of garbage," says Coyote.

"Try again," says the pillow.

"A warm pile of moose poop?"

"Nope."

"A skunk?" says Coyote.

"Right!" says Skunk, and sprays Coyote all over with really bad-smelling skunk business.

"EEEEYOOOOW!" yells Coyote, and he jumps up and runs off as fast as he can. He runs and runs and runs and runs.

And runs right off a cliff.

"Oops!" says Coyote. "I can't watch. . . . ." And Coyote closes his eyes and holds onto his tail as he falls and falls and falls.

And falls right into the pond.

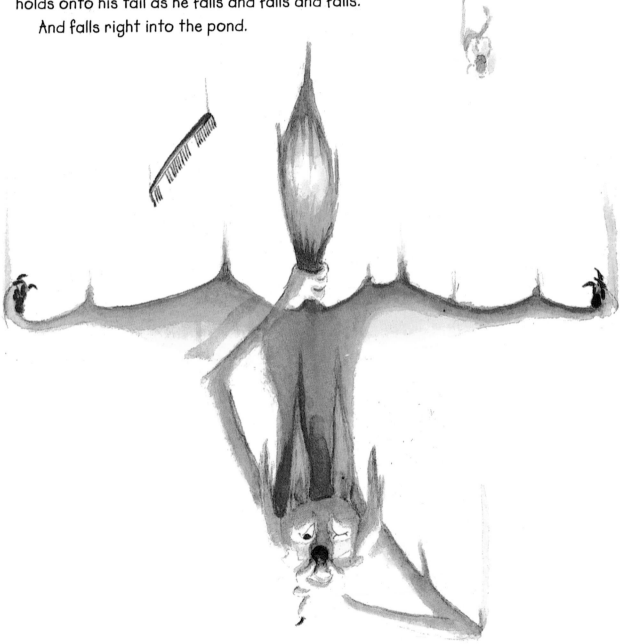

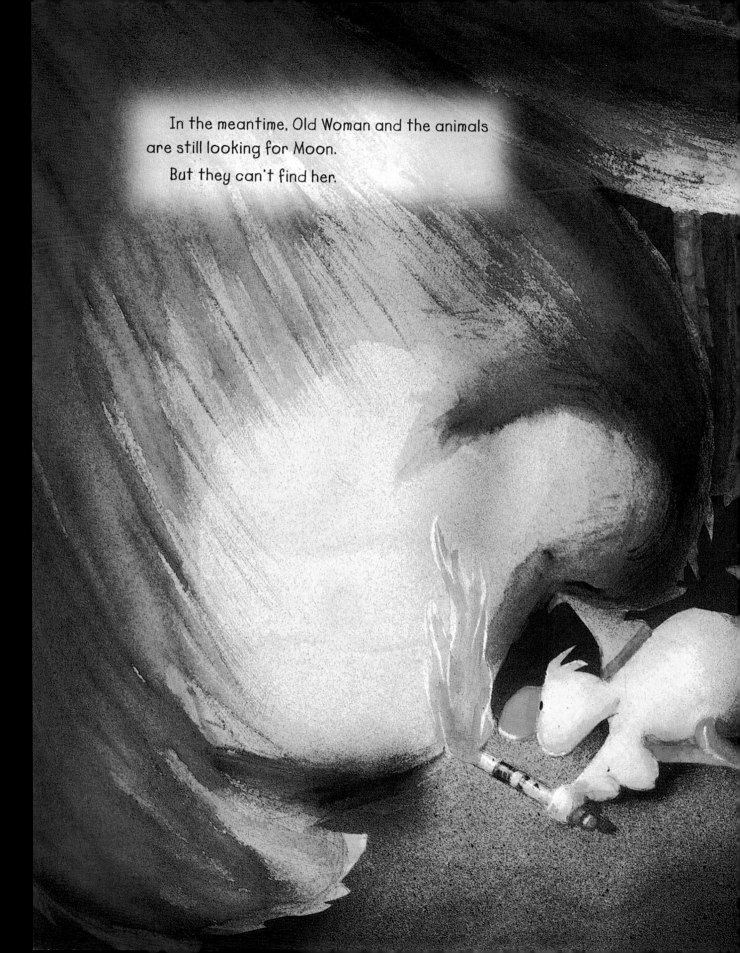

In the meantime, Old Woman and the animals
are still looking for Moon.
But they can't find her.

"Did you look in that old hollow tree?" says Old Woman.

"We looked there," say the squirrels.

"Did you look in the cave?"

"Yes," say the bears. "We looked there, too."

"Maybe she's hiding behind the waterfall," says Old Woman.

"No," say the deer, "she's not there."

Old Woman sits down on a rock and puts her head in her hand. "Now, where could that Moon be?"

When Coyote opens his eyes, he is at the bottom of the pond.

"Oh dear," says Coyote. "This is embarrassing."

Then he notices something curious. Instead of being cold and dark at the bottom of the pond, it is nice and bright.

"Hmmmm," says Coyote. "This is very curious."

Coyote walks along the bottom of the pond a little ways, and there, lying on a beach towel under a beach umbrella, playing chess with a sunfish, is Moon.

"There you are," cries Coyote.

"Go away," says Moon. "I've almost won this game."

"Checkmate!" says Sunfish, taking Moon's knight with his bishop. "Good grief, what stinks?"

"Never mind," says Coyote.

"Let's play again," says Moon, wrinkling her nose. "Phew, what stinks?"

"Never mind," says Coyote. "You have to get back up in the sky."

"I like it here," says Moon. "But you have to get back up in the sky," says Coyote.

"Have you noticed that you're underwater?" says Moon.

"Oh boy," Coyote thinks to himself. "I better get some help. I better get some air!"

Old Woman and all the animals are sitting at the edge of the pond, feeling glum, when Coyote pops out of the water.

"You again!" says Old Woman.

"Relax," says Coyote. "I've found Moon. She's at the bottom of the pond."

Old Woman and all the animals put their heads into the pond, and, sure enough, there's Moon playing chess with Sunfish.

"This is a fine mess you've made," Old Woman tells Coyote. "Now what are we going to do?"

So Coyote and the animals and Old Woman sit on the grass by the pond in the dark and think.

After a while, Old Woman stands up. "All right," she says. "First, we have to build a raft."

So all of the next day, when they can see what they are doing, Old Woman and the animals and Coyote build a raft. And just before the sun disappears, everybody gets on the raft and they float out to where Moon is lounging on the bottom of the pond.

"All right," says Old Woman, "everybody sing. Everybody, that is, except Coyote."

"That's not very nice," says Coyote. "After all, I found Moon."

"Just sit there and be quiet," says Old Woman.

Old Woman begins to sing first. "Moon, Moon, come back soon."

And then, one by one, all the animals join in. "Moon, Moon, come back soon."

They sing for hours and hours. "Moon, Moon, come back soon." But nothing happens. And when Old Woman looks underwater, Moon is still playing chess and relaxing on the beach blanket under the beach umbrella.

"Okay," says Old Woman, "now we get serious."

Old Woman moves all the animals off to one side of the raft. "Stop singing," she says, "and put your fingers in your ears."

"Okay," say all the animals.

Old Woman tries to smile at Coyote. "I was wrong about your singing." she says. "You have a beautiful voice, and I think if you sing all by yourself, Moon will go back up in the sky."

"A solo?" says Coyote, trying to keep his tongue from falling out of his head.

"But you have to sing really loud," says Old Woman.

"I'll sing really, really loud," says Coyote.

"But," says Old Woman, "don't sing until I give you the signal."

Coyote takes out his comb and brushes his coat. He runs his tongue over his teeth and wipes his nose on his arm.

Old Woman sits on the raft with the animals and puts her fingers in her ears. "Okay," she says, closing her eyes, "hit it."

Coyote sits up straight, points his nose at the stars, opens his mouth, and begins to sing.

"YEEOO-EEEOOO-WAAAAH-YOOOOOO!"

"Yikes!" scream Old Woman and all the animals.

"YOOOO-EEEEEYOOOOOOOW-YOOOWWWWW!" sings Coyote.

"Stop! Stop!" scream Old Woman and all the animals. "It's worse than we thought."

But Coyote doesn't hear them. He keeps right on singing.

Down at the bottom of the pond, Moon is just about to take Sunfish's queen with her rook when she hears Coyote.

"What is that awful noise?" says Moon.

"It's a good thing I don't have ears," says Sunfish.

Coyote's singing gets louder and louder. Moon puts her fingers in her ears, but it doesn't help.

"Who is making that horrible noise?" says Moon, and she packs up her umbrella and her blanket and swims to the top of the pond to see what is happening.

When Old Woman sees Moon coming to the surface, she yells at Coyote, "Sing louder!"

Just as Moon comes out of the water and looks around, Coyote takes a deep breath and sings as loud as he can.

"AAAAWOOOOOOOOO, AAAWOOOOOOOOOOOOOO!"

"AAAGGGGGGH!" screams Moon, and she leaps up into the sky.

"AAAAWWWOOOOOO," sings Coyote. "EEEEYOOOOOOOOOWW!"

Moon climbs into the sky as fast as she can, trying to get away from Coyote's singing.

"Enough!" yells Old Woman.

But Coyote doesn't hear her
and he keeps on singing, and Moon
keeps on climbing.

Old Woman can see that if she doesn't shut Coyote up, Moon will climb into the sky until she disappears. So, quick as she can, Old Woman grabs Coyote's tongue and wraps it around his mouth so he can't sing anymore.

But Coyote's tongue is long and slippery, and by the time she has Coyote's mouth all wrapped, Moon is much farther away than before and the light from Moon is very dim.

"Oh dear," says Old Woman. "This didn't exactly work out the way I planned."

"Wouya pwease umwapp ma tongue," says Coyote, with his tongue wrapped around his mouth.

"But I guess it will have to do," says Old Woman.

"Anything to keep Coyote from singing," say the animals.

But just then, Moon begins sneaking out of the sky toward that pond.

"Look out, look out," all the animals yell to Old Woman. "Moon is sneaking out of the sky."

Old Woman looks up. Moon is picking up speed, heading for that pond. Old Woman grabs Coyote's tongue and unwraps his mouth.

"Start singing," she shouts.

"Are you going to wrap my tongue around my mouth again?" says Coyote.

"Just sing," says Old Woman.

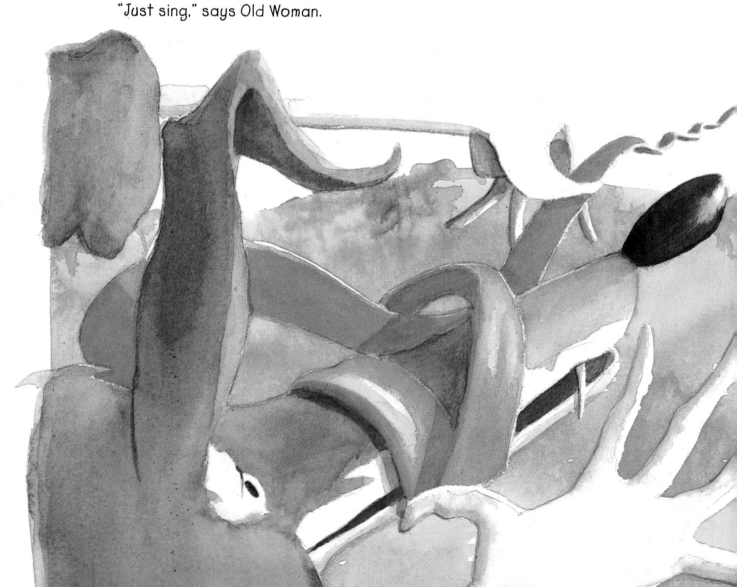

So Coyote starts to sing again. "EYOOOOOOOOOW, AWOUUUUUUUUU!"

And as soon as Moon hears Coyote start to sing, she turns around and heads back up in the sky.

"Well," says Old Woman, "this is a fine mess."

"I have an idea," says Coyote. "I'll watch Moon every night, and whenever she tries to sneak back to the pond, I'll sing to her."

"Oh, no," say all the animals.

"Oh, no," says Old Woman.

But it's the only way to keep Moon in the sky.

So every evening, when Old Woman walks down to the pond to watch Moon come up, Coyote sits on a hill and waits. He combs his fur, runs his tongue around his teeth, and wipes his nose on his arm.

"Awoooooooo," he sings softly to himself, just to stay in good voice. "Awwwwooooooooo."